Jules Verne

A Voyage in a Balloon

Outlook

Jules Verne

A Voyage in a Balloon

1. Auflage | ISBN: 978-3-73262-421-8

Erscheinungsort: Frankfurt am Main, Deutschland

Erscheinungsjahr: 2018

Outlook Verlag GmbH, Frankfurt.

Jules Verne

A Voyage in a Balloon

Outlook

A VOYAGE IN A BALLOON

by

Jules Verne

Translated from the French by Anne T. Wilbur

1852

I.

My Ascension at Frankfort—The Balloon, the Gas, the
Apparatus, the Ballast—An Unexpected Travelling
Companion—Conversation in the Air—Anecdotes—At
800 Metres [A] —The Portfolio of the Pale Young Man—
Pictures and Caricatures—Des Rosiers and d'Arlandes—
At 1200 Metres—Atmospheric Phenomena—The
Philosopher Charles—Systems—Blanchard—Guyton-
Morveaux—M. Julien—M. Petin—At 1500 Metres—The
Storm—Great Personages in Balloons—The Valve—The
Curious Animals—The Aerial Ship—Game of Balloons.

[A] A metre is equal to 39.33 English inches.

In the month of September, 1850, I arrived at Frankfort-on-the-
Maine. My passage through the principal cities of Germany, had been
brilliantly marked by aerostatic ascensions; but, up to this day, no
inhabitant of the Confederation had accompanied me, and the
successful experiments at Paris of Messrs. Green, Godard, and
Poitevin, had failed to induce the grave Germans to attempt aerial
voyages.

Meanwhile, hardly had the news of my approaching ascension
circulated throughout Frankfort, than three persons of note asked the

favour of accompanying me. Two days after, we were to ascend from the Place de la Comédie. I immediately occupied myself with the preparations. My balloon, of gigantic proportions, was of silk, coated with gutta percha, a substance not liable to injury from acids or gas, and of absolute impermeability. Some trifling rents were mended: the inevitable results of perilous descents.

The day of our ascension was that of the great fair of September, which attracts all the world to Frankfort. The apparatus for filling was composed of six hogsheads arranged around a large vat, hermetically sealed. The hydrogen gas, evolved by the contact of water with iron and sulphuric acid, passed from the first reservoirs to the second, and thence into the immense globe, which was thus graduallyinflated. These preparations occupied all the morning, and about 11 o'clock, the balloon was three-quarters full; sufficiently so;—for as we rise, the atmospheric layers diminish in density, and the gas, confined within the aerostat, acquiring more elasticity, might otherwise burst its envelope. My calculations had furnished me with the exact measurement of gas required to carry my companions and myself to a considerable height.

We were to ascend at noon. It was truly a magnificent spectacle, that of the impatient crowd who thronged around the reserved enclosure, inundated the entire square and adjoining streets, and covered the neighbouring houses from the basements to the slated roofs. The high winds of past days had lulled, and an overpowering heat was radiating from an unclouded sky; not a breath animated the atmosphere. In such weather, one might descend in the very spot he had left.

I carried three hundred pounds of ballast, in bags; the car, perfectly round, four feet in diameter, and three feet in height, was conveniently attached; the cord which sustained it was symmetrically extended from the upper hemisphere of the aerostat; the compass was in its place, the barometer suspended to the iron hoop which surrounded the supporting cord, at a distance of eight feet above the car; the anchor carefully prepared;—all was in readiness for our departure.

Among the persons who crowded around the enclosure, I remarked a young man with pale face and agitated features. I was struck with his appearance. He had been an assiduous spectator of my ascensions in several cities of Germany. His uneasy air and his extraordinary pre-occupation never left him; he eagerly contemplated the curious machine, which rested motionless at a few feet from the ground, and remained silent.

The clock struck twelve! This was the hour. My *compagnons du voyage* had not appeared. I sent to the dwelling of each, and learned that one had started for Hamburg, another for Vienna and the third, still more fearful, for London. Their hearts had failed them at the moment of undertaking one of those excursions, which, since the ingenious experiments of aeronauts, are deprived of all danger. As they made, as it were a part of the programme of the fête, they had feared being compelled to fulfil their agreements, and had fled at the moment of ascension. Their courage had been in inverse ratio to the square of their swiftness in retreat.

The crowd, thus partly disappointed, were shouting with anger and impatience. I did not hesitate to ascend alone. To re-establish the equilibrium between the specific gravity of the balloon and the weight to be raised, I substituted other bags of sand for my expected companions and entered the car. The twelve men who were holding the aerostat by twelve cords fastened to the equatorial circle, let them slip between their fingers; the car rose a few feet above the ground. There was not a breath of wind, and the atmosphere, heavy as lead, seemed insurmountable.

"All is ready!" exclaimed I; "attention!"

The men arranged themselves; a last glance informed me that everything was right.

"Attention!"

There was some movement in the crowd which seemed to be invading the reserved enclosure.

"Let go!"

The balloon slowly ascended; but I experienced a shock which threw me to the bottom of the car. When I rose, I found myself face to face with an unexpected voyager,—the pale young man.

"Monsieur, I salute you!" said he to me.

"By what right?"—

"Am I here? By the right of your inability to turn me out."

I was confounded. His assurance disconcerted me; and I had nothing to say in reply. I looked at him, but he paid no regard to my astonishment. He continued:

"My weight will disturb your equilibrium, Monsieur: will you permit me—"

3

And without waiting for my assent, he lightened the balloon by two bags of sand which he emptied into the air.

"Monsieur," said I, taking the only possible course, "you are here,—well! you choose to remain,—well! but to me alone belongs the management of the aerostat."

"Monsieur," replied he, "your urbanity is entirely French; it is of the same country with myself! I press in imagination the hand which you refuse me. Take your measures,—act as it may seem good to you; I will wait till you have ended—"

"To—"

"To converse with you."

The barometer had fallen to twenty-six inches; we had attained a height of about six hundred metres, and were over the city; which satisfied me of our complete quiescence, for I could not judge by our motionless flags. Nothing betrays the horizontal voyage of a balloon; it is the mass of air surrounding it which moves. A kind of wavering heat bathed the objects extended at our feet, and gave their outlines an indistinctness to be regretted. The needle of the compass indicated a slight tendency to float towards the south.

I looked again at my companion. He was a man of thirty, simply clad; the bold outlines of his features betokened indomitable energy; he appeared very muscular. Absorbed in the emotion of this silent suspension, he remained immovable, seeking to distinguish the objects which passed beneath his view.

"Vexatious mist!" said he, at the expiration of a few moments.

I made no reply.

"What would you? I could not pay for my voyage; I was obliged to take you by surprise."

"No one has asked you to descend!"

"A similar occurrence," he resumed, "happened to the Counts of Laurencin and Dampierre, when they ascended at Lyons, on the 15th of January, 1784. A young merchant, named Fontaine, scaled the railing, at the risk of upsetting the equipage. He accomplished the voyage, and nobody was killed!"

"Once on the earth, we will converse!" said I, piqued at the tone of lightness with which he spoke.

4

"Bah! do not talk of returning!"

"Do you think then that I shall delay my descent?"

"Descent!" said he, with surprise. "Let us ascend!"

And before I could prevent him, two bags of sand were thrown out, without even being emptied.

"Monsieur!" said I, angrily.

"I know your skill," replied he, composedly; "your brilliant ascensions have made some noise in the world. Experience is the sister of practice, but it is also first cousin to theory, and I have long and deeply studied the aerostatic art. It has affected my brain," added he, sadly, falling into a mute torpor.

The balloon, after having risen, remained stationary; the unknown consulted the barometer, and said:

"Here we are at 800 metres! Men resemble insects! See, I think it is from this height that we should always look at them, to judge correctly of their moral proportions! The Place de la Comédie is transformed to an immense ant-hill. Look at the crowd piled up on the quays. The Zeil diminishes. We are above the church of Dom. The Mein is now only a white line dividing the city, and this bridge, the Mein-Brucke, looks like a white thread thrown between the two banks of the river."

The atmosphere grew cooler.

"There is nothing I will not do for you, my host," said my companion. "If you are cold, I will take off my clothes and lend them to you."

"Thanks!"

"Necessity makes laws. Give me your hand, I am your countryman. You shall be instructed by my company, and my conversation shall compensate you for the annoyance I have caused you."

I seated myself, without replying, at the opposite extremity of the car. The young man had drawn from his great coat a voluminous portfolio; it was a work on aerostation.

"I possess," said he, "a most curious collection of engraving, and caricatures appertaining to our aerial mania. This precious discovery has been at once admired and ridiculed. Fortunately we have passed the period when the Mongolfiers sought to make factitious clouds with the vapour of water; and of the gas affecting electric properties, which they produced by the combustion of damp straw with chopped wool."

"Would you detract from the merit of these inventions?" replied I. "Was it not well done to have proved by experiment the possibility of rising in the air?"

"Who denies the glory of the first aerial navigators? Immense courage was necessary to ascend by means of those fragile envelopes which contained only warm air. Besides, has not aerostatic science made great progress since the ascensions of Blanchard? Look, Monsieur."

He took from his collection an engraving.

"Here is the first aerial voyage undertaken by Pilatre des Rosiers and the Marquis d'Arlandes, four months after the discovery of balloons. Louis XVI. refused his consent to this voyage; two condemned criminals were to have first attempted aerial travelling. Pilatre des Rosiers was indignant at this injustice and, by means of artifice, succeeded in setting out. This car, which renders the management of the balloon easy, had not then been invented; a circular gallery surrounded the lower part of the aerostat. The two aeronauts stationed themselves at the extremities of this gallery. The damp straw with which it was filled encumbered their movements. A chafing-dish was suspended beneath the orifice of the balloon; when the voyagers wished to ascend, they threw, with a long fork, straw upon this brazier, at the risk of burning the machine, and the air, growing warmer, gave to the balloon a new ascensional force. The two bold navigators ascended, on the 21st of November, 1783, from the gardens of La Muette, which the Dauphin had placed at their disposal. The aerostat rose majestically, passed the Isle des Cygnes, crossed the Seine at the Barrière de la Conference, and, directing its way between the dome of the Invalides and L'Ecole Militaire, approached St. Sulpice; then the aeronauts increased the fire, ascended, cleared the Boulevard, and descended beyond the Barrière d'Enfer. As it touched the ground, the collapsed, and buried Pilatre des Rosiers beneath its folds."

"Unfortunate presage!" said I, interested in these details, which so nearly concerned me.

"Presage of his catastrophe," replied the unknown, with sadness. "You have experienced nothing similar?"

"Nothing!"

"Bah! misfortunes often arrive without presage." And he remained silent.

We were advancing towards the south; the magnetic needle pointed in the direction of Frankfort, which was flying beneath our feet.

"Perhaps we shall have a storm," said the young man.

"We will descend first."

"Indeed! it will be better to ascend; we shall escape more surely;" and two bags of sand were thrown overboard.

The balloon rose rapidly, and stopped at twelve hundred metres. The cold was now intense, and there was a slight buzzing in my ears. Nevertheless, the rays of the sun fell hotly on the globe, and, dilating the gas it contained, gave it a greater ascensional force. I was stupified.

"Fear nothing," said the young man to me.

"We have three thousand five hundred toises of respirable air. You need not trouble yourself about my proceedings."

I would have risen, but a vigorous hand detained me on my seat.

"Your name?" asked I.

"My name! how does it concern you?"

"I have the honour to ask your name."

"I am called Erostratus or Empedocles,—as you please. Are you interested in the progress of aerostatic science?"

He spoke with icy coldness, and I asked myself with whom I had to do.

"Monsieur," continued he, "nothing new has been invented since the days of the philosopher Charles. Four months after the discovery of aerostats, he had invented the valve, which permits the gas to escape when the balloon is too full, or when one wishes to descend; the car, which allows the machine to be easily managed; the network, which encloses the fabric of the balloon, and prevents its being too heavily pressed; the ballast, which is used in ascending and choosing the spot of descent; the coat of caoutchouc, which renders the silk impermeable; the barometer, which determines the height attained; and, finally, the hydrogen, which, fourteen times lighter than air, allows of ascension to the most distant atmospheric layers, and prevents exposure to aerial combustion. On the 1st of December, 1783, three hundred thousand spectators thronged the Tuileries. Charles ascended, and the soldiers presented arms. He travelled nine leagues in the air: managing his machine with a skill never since surpassed in aeronautic experiments. The King conferred on him a pension of two thousand livres, for in those days inventions were encouraged. In a few days, the subscription list was filled; for every one was interested in the progress of science."

The unknown was seized with a violent agitation.

"I, Monsieur, have studied; I am satisfied that the first aeronauts guided their balloons. Not to speak of Blanchard, whose assertions might be doubted, at Dijon, Guyton-Morveaux, by the aid of oars and a helm, imparted to his machines perceptible motions, a decided direction. More recently, at Paris, a watchmaker, M. Julien, has made at the Hippodrome convincing experiments; for, with the aid of a particular mechanism, an aerial apparatus of oblong form was manifestly propelled against the wind. M. Petin placed four balloons, filled with hydrogen, in juxtaposition, and, by means of sails disposed horizontally and partially furled, hoped to obtain a disturbance of the equilibrium, which, inclining the apparatus, should compel it to an oblique path. But the motive power destined to surmount the resistance of currents,—the helice, moving in a movable medium, was unsuccessful. I have discovered the only method of guiding balloons, and not an Academy has come to my assistance, not a city has filled my subscription lists, not a government has deigned to listen to me! It is infamous!"

His gesticulations were so furious that the car experienced violent oscillations; I had much difficulty in restraining him. Meanwhile, the balloon had encountered a more rapid current. We were advancing in a southerly direction, at 1200 metres in height, almost accustomed to this new temperature.

"There is Darmstadt," said my companion. "Do you perceive its magnificent chateau? The storm-cloud below makes the outlines of objects waver; and it requires a practised eye to recognise localities."

"You are certain that it is Darmstadt?"

"Undoubtedly; we are six leagues from Frankfort."

"Then we must descend."

"Descend! you would not alight upon the steeples!" said the unknown, mockingly.

"No; but in the environs of the city."

"Well, it is too warm; let us remount a little."

As he spoke thus, he seized some bags of ballast. I precipitated myself upon him; but, with one hand, he overthrew me, and the lightened balloon rose to a height of 1500 metres.

"Sit down," said he, "and do not forget that Brioschi, Biot, and Gay-Lussac, ascended to a height of seven thousand metres, in order to establish some new scientific laws."

"We must descend;" resumed I, with an attempt at gentleness. "The storm is gathering beneath our feet and around us; it would not be prudent."

"We will ascend above it, and shall have nothing to fear from it. What more beautiful than to reign in heaven, and look down upon the clouds which hover upon the earth! Is it not an honour to navigate these aerial waves? The greatest personages have travelled like ourselves. The Marquise and Comtesse de Montalembert, the Comtesse de Potteries, Mlle. La Garde, the Marquis of Montalembert, set out from the Faubourg St. Antoine for these unknown regions. The Duc de Chartres displayed much address and presence of mind in his ascension of the 15th of July, 1784; at Lyons, the Comtes de Laurencin and de Dampierre; at Nantes, M. de Luynes; at Bordeaux, D'Arbelet des Granges; in Italy, the Chevalier Andreani; in our days, the Duke of Brunswick; have left in the air the track of their glory. In order to equal these great personages, we must ascend into the celestial regions higher than they. To approach the infinite is to comprehend it."

The rarefaction of the air considerably dilated the hydrogen, and I saw the lower part of the aerostat, designedly left empty, become by degrees inflated, rendering the opening of the valve indispensable; but my fearful companion seemed determined not to allow me to direct our movements. I resolved to pull secretly the cord attached to the valve, while he was talking with animation. I feared to guess with whom I had to do; it would have been too horrible! It was about three-quarters of an hour since we had left Frankfort, and from the south thick clouds were arising and threatening to engulf us.

"Have you lost all hope of making your plans succeed?" said I, with great apparent interest.

"All hope!" replied the unknown, despairingly. "Wounded by refusals, caricatures, those blows with the foot of an ass, have finished me. It is the eternal punishment reserved for innovators. See these caricatures of every age with which my portfolio is filled."

I had secured the cord of the valve, and stooping over his works, concealed my movements from him. It was to be feared, nevertheless, that he would notice that rushing sound, like a waterfall, which the gas produces in escaping.

"How many jests at the expense of the Abbé Miolan! He was about to ascend with Janninet and Bredin. During the operation, their balloon took fire, and an ignorant populace tore it to pieces. Then the caricature of *The Curious Animals* called them *Maulant, Jean Mind, and Gredin.*"

The barometer had began to rise; it was time! A distant muttering of thunder was heard towards the south.

"See this other engraving," continued he, without seeming to suspect my manoeuvres. "It is an immense balloon, containing a ship, large castles, houses, &c. The caricaturists little thought that their absurdities would one day become verities. It is a large vessel; at the left is the helm with the pilot's box; at the prow, *maisons de plaisance*, a gigantic organ, and cannon to call the attention of the inhabitants of earth or of the moon; above the stern the observatory and pilot-balloon; at the equatorial circle, the barracks of the army; on the left the lantern; then upper galleries for promenades, the sails, the wings; beneath, the cafés and general store-houses of provisions. Admire this magnificent announcement. 'Invented for the good of the human race, this globe will depart immediately for the seaports in the Levant, and on its return will announce its voyages for the two poles and the extremities of the Occident. Every provision is made; there will be an exact rate of fare for each place of destination; but the prices for distant voyages will be the same, 1000 louis. And it must be confessed that this is a moderate sum, considering the celerity, convenience, and pleasure of this mode of travelling above all others. While in this balloon, every one can divert himself as he pleases, dancing, playing, or conversing with people of talent. Pleasure will be the soul of the aerial society.' All these inventions excited laughter. But before long, if my days were not numbered, these projects should become realities."

We were visibly descending; he did not perceive it!

"See this game of balloons; it contains the whole history of the aerostatic art. This game, for the use of educated minds, is played like that of the Jew; with dice and counters of any value agreed upon, which are to be paid or received, according to the condition in which one arrives."

"But," I resumed, "you seem to have valuable documents on aerostation?"

"I am less learned than the Almighty! That is all! I possess all the knowledge possible in this world. From Phaeton, Icarus, and Architas. I have searched all, comprehended all! Through me, the aerostatic art would render immense services to the world, if God should spare my life! But that cannot be."

"Why not?"

"Because my name is Empedocles or Erostratus!"

II.

The Company of Aerostiers—The Battle of Fleurus—The Balloon over the Sea—Blanchard and Jefferies—A Drama such as is rarely seen—3000 Metres—The Thunder beneath our Feet—Gavnerin at Rome—The Compass gone—The Victims of Aerostation—Pilatre—At 4000 Metres—The Barometer gone—Descents of Olivari, Mosment, Bittorf, Harris, Sadler, and Madame Blanchard—The Valve rendered useless—7000 Metres— Zambecarri—The Ballon (sic) Wrecked—Incalculable Heights—The Car Overset—Despair—Vertigo—The Fall —The Dénouement.

I shuddered! Fortunately the balloon was approaching the earth. But the danger is the same at 50 feet as at 5000 metres! The clouds were advancing.

"Remember the battle of Fleurus, and you will comprehend the utility of aerostats! Coulee, by order of the government, organized a company of aerostiers. At the siege of Maubeuge, General Jourdan found this new method of observation so serviceable, that twice a day, accompanied by the General himself, Coutelle ascended into the air; the correspondence between the aeronaut and the aerostiers who held the balloon, was carried on by means of little white, red, and yellow flags. Cannons and carbines were often aimed at the balloon at the moment of its ascension, but without effect. When Jourdan was preparing to invest Charleroi, Coutelle repaired to the neighbourhood of that place, rose from the plain of Jumet, and remained taking observations seven or eight hours, with General Morelot. The Austrians came to deliver the city, and a battle was fought on the heights of Fleurus. General Jourdan publicly proclaimed the assistance he had received from aeronautic observations. Well! notwithstanding the services rendered on this occasion, and during the campaign with Belgium, the year which witnessed the commencement of the military career of balloons, also saw it terminate. And the school of Meuon, founded by government, was closed by Bonaparte, on his return from Egypt. 'What are we to expect from the child which has just been born?' Franklin had said. But the child was born alive! It need not have been strangled!"

The unknown hid his forehead in his hands, reflected for a few moments, then, without raising his head, said to me:

"Notwithstanding my orders, you have opened the upper valve!"

I let go the cord.

"Fortunately" continued he, "we have still two hundred pounds of ballast."

"What are your plans?" said I, with effort.

"You have never crossed the sea?"

I grew frightfully pale, terror froze my veins.

"It is a pity," said he, "that we are being wafted towards the Adriatic! That is only a streamlet. Higher! we shall find other currents!"

And without looking at me, he lightened the balloon by several bags of sand.

"I allowed you to open the valve, because the dilatation of the gas threatened to burst the balloon. But do not do it again."

I was stupified.

"You know the voyage from Dover to Calais made by Blanchard and Jefferies. It was rich in incident. On the 7th of January, 1785, in a northeast wind, their balloon was filled with gas on the Dover side; scarcely had they risen, when an error in equilibrium compelled them to threw out their ballast, retaining only thirty pounds. The wind drifted them slowly along towards the shores of France. The permeability of the tissue gradually suffered the gas to escape, and at the expiration of an hour and a half, the voyagers perceived that they were descending. 'What is to be done?' said Jefferies.—'We have passed over only three-fourths of the distance,' replied Blanchard 'and at a slight elevation. By ascending we shall expose ourselves to contrary winds. Throw out the remainder of the ballast.' The balloon regained its ascensional force, but soon re-descended. About midway of the voyage, the aeronauts threw out their books and tools. A quarter of an hour afterwards, Blanchard said to Jefferies: 'The barometer?'— 'It is rising! We are lost; and yet there are the shores of France!' A great noise was heard. 'Is the balloon rent?' asked Jefferies. —'No! the escape of the gas has collapsed the lower part of the balloon'—'But we are still descending. We are lost! Everything not indispensable must be thrown overboard!' Their provisions, oars and helm were thrown out into the sea. They were now only 100 metres in height. 'We are remounting,' said the Doctor.—' No, it is the jerk caused by the diminution of weight. There is not a ship in sight! Not a bark on the horizon! To the sea with our garments!' And the unfortunate men stripped, but the balloon continued to descend. 'Blanchard,' said Jefferies, 'you were to have made this voyage alone; you consented to take me; I will sacrifice myself to you! I will throw myself into the water, and the balloon, relieved, will re-ascend!'—' No, no, it is frightful.' The balloon collapsed more and more, and its concavity forming a parachute, forced the gas against its sides and accelerated its motion. 'Adieu, my friend,' said the Doctor. 'May God preserve you!' He was about to have taken the leap, when Blanchard detained him. 'One resource remains to us! We can cut the cords by which the car is attached, and cling to the network? perhaps the balloon will rise. Ready! But the barometer falls! We remount! The wind freshens! We are saved!' The voyagers perceived Calais! Their joy became delirium; a few moments later, they descended in the forest of Guines. I doubt not," continued the unknown, "that in similar circumstances you would follow the example of Doctor Jefferies."

The clouds were unrolling beneath our feet in glittering cascades; the balloon cast a deep shadow on this pile of clouds, and was surrounded by them as with an aureola! The thunder growled beneath our feet! All this was frightful!

"Let us descend!" exclaimed I.

"Descend, when the sun is awaiting us yonder! Down with the bags!" And he lightened the balloon of more than fifty pounds. At 3000 metres we remained stationary. The unknown talked incessantly, but I scarcely heard him; I was completely prostrated, while he seemed in his element.

"With a good wind, we shall go far, but we must especially go high!"

"We are lost!"

"In the Antilles there are currents of air which travel a hundred leagues an hour! On the occasion of Napoleon's coronation, Gavnerin let off a balloon illuminated with coloured lamps, at eleven o'clock in the evening! The wind blew from the N.N.E.; the next morning at daybreak the inhabitants of Rome saluted its passage above the dome of St. Peter's. We will go farther."

I scarcely heard him; everything was buzzing around me! There was an opening in the clouds!

"See that city, my host;" said the unknown. "It is Spire. Nothing else!"

I dared not lean over the railing of the car. Nevertheless I perceived a little black spot. This was Spire. The broad Rhine looked like a riband, the great roads like threads. Above our heads the sky was of a deep azure; I was benumbed with the cold. The birds had long since forsaken us; in this rarefied air their flight would have been impossible. We were alone in space, and I in the presence of a strange man!

"It is useless for you to know whither I am taking you," said he, and he threw the compass into the clouds. "A fall is a fine thing. You know that there have been a few victims from Pilatre des Rosiers down to Lieutenant Gale, and these misfortunes have always been caused by imprudence. Pilatre des Rosiers ascended in company with Remain, at Boulogne, on the 13th of June, 1785. To his balloon, inflated with gas, he had suspended a *mongolfier* filled with warm air, undoubtedly to save the trouble of letting off gas, or throwing out ballast. It was like putting a chafing-dish beneath a powder-cask. The imprudent men rose to a height of four hundred metres, and encountered opposing winds, which drove them over the ocean. In order to descend, Pilatre attempted to open the valve of the aerostat; but the cord of this valve caught in the balloon, and tore it so that it was emptied in an instant. It fell on the mongolfier, overturned it, and the imprudent men were dashed to pieces in a few seconds. It is frightful, is it not?" said the unknown, shaking me from my torpor.

I could reply only by these words:

"In pity, let us descend! The clouds are gathering around us in every direction, and frightful detonations reverberating from the cavity of the aerostat are multiplying around us."

"You make me impatient!" said he. "You shall no longer know whether we are ascending or descending."

And the barometer went after the compass, along with some bags of sand. We must have been at a height of four thousand metres. Some icicles were attached to the sides of the car, and a sort of fine snow penetrated to my bones. Meanwhile a terrific storm was bursting beneath our feet. We were above it.

"Do not fear," said my strange companion; "it is only imprudence that makes victims. Olivari, who perished at Orleans, ascended in a mongolfier made of paper; his car, suspended below the chafing-dish, and ballasted with combustible materials, became a prey to the flames! Olivari fell, and was killed. Mosment ascended at Lille, on a light platform; an oscillation made him lose his equilibrium. Mosment fell, and was killed. Bittorf, at Manheim, saw his paper balloon take fire in the air! Bittorf fell, and was killed. Harris ascended in a balloon badly constructed, the valve of which was too large to be closed again. Harris fell, and was killed. Sadler, deprived of ballast by his long stay in the air, was dragged over the city of Boston, and thrown against the chimneys. Sadler fell, and was killed. Cocking descended with a convex parachute which he pretended to have perfected. Cocking fell, and was killed. Well, I love them, those noble victims of their courage! and I will die like them! Higher! higher!"

All the phantoms of this necrology were passing before my eyes! The rarefaction of the air and the rays of tile sun increased the dilatation of the gas; the balloon continued to ascend! I mechanically attempted to open the valve; but the unknown cut the cord a few feet above my head. I was lost!

"Did you see Madame Blanchard fall?" said he to me. "I saw her, I— yes, I was at Tivoli on the 6th of July, 1819. Madame Blanchard ascended in a balloon of small size, to save the expense of filling; she was therefore obliged to inflate it entirely, and the gas escaped by the lower orifice, leaving on its route a train of hydrogen. She carried, suspended above her car, by an iron wire, a kind of firework, forming an aureola, which she was to kindle. She had often repeated this experiment. On this occasion she carried, besides, a little parachute, ballasted by a firework terminating in a ball with silver rain. She was to launch this apparatus, after having lighted it with a *lance à feu*, prepared for the purpose. She ascended. The night was dark. At the moment of lighting the firework, she was so imprudent as to let the lance pass beneath the column of hydrogen, which was escaping from the balloon. My eyes were fixed on her. Suddenly an unexpected flash illuminated the darkness. I thought it a surprise of the skilful aeronaut.

The flame increased, suddenly disappeared, and re-appeared at the top of the aerostat under the form of an immense jet of burning gas. This sinister light projected over the Boulevard, and over the quarter Montmartre. Then I saw the unfortunate woman rise, twice attempt to compress the orifice of the balloon, to extinguish the fire, then seat herself in the car and seek to direct its descent; for she did not fall. The combustion of the gas lasted several minutes. The balloon, diminishing by degrees, continued to descend, but this was not a fall! The wind blew from the northeast, and drove her over Paris. There were, at that time, in the neighbourhood of the house No. 16 Rue de Provence, immense gardens. The aeronaut might have fallen there without danger. But unhappily the balloon and the car alighted on the roof of the house. The shock was slight. 'Help!' cried the unfortunate woman. I arrived in the street at that moment. The car slid along the roof, and encountered an iron hook. At this shock, Madame Blanchard was thrown out of the car, and precipitated on the pavement! She was killed!"

These histories of fatal augury froze me with horror. The unknown was standing upright, with bare head, bristling hair, haggard eyes.

Illusion was no longer possible. I saw at last the horrible truth. I had to deal with a madman!

He threw out half the ballast, and we must have been borne to a height of 7000 metres! Blood spouted from my nose and mouth.

"What a fine thing it is to be martyrs to science! They are canonized by posterity!"

I heard no more. The unknown looked around him with horror, and knelt at my ear.

"On the 7th of October, 1804, the weather had began to clear up a little; for several days preceding, the wind and rain had been incessant. But the ascension announced by Zambecarri could not be postponed! His idiot enemies already scoffed at him. To save himself and science from public ridicule, it became necessary for him to ascend. It was at Bologna! No one aided him in filling his balloon; he rose at midnight, accompanied by Andreoli and Grossetti. The balloon ascended slowly; it had been rent by the wind, and the gas escaped. The three intrepid voyagers could observe the state of the barometer only by the aid of a dark lantern. Zambecarri had not eaten during twenty-four hours; Grossetti was also fasting.

"'My friends,' said Zambecarri, 'I am benumbed with the cold; I am exhausted; I must die;' and he fell senseless in the gallery.

"It was the same with Grossetti. Andreoli alone remained awake. After long efforts he succeeded in arousing Zambecarri from his stupor.

"'What is there new? Where are we going? In which direction is the wind? What time is it?'

"' It is two o'clock!'

"' Where is the compass?'

"'It has fallen out.'

"' Great God! the lamp is extinguished!'

"' It could not burn longer in this rarefied air!' said Zambecarri.

"The moon had not risen; the atmosphere was plunged in horrible darkness.

"' I am cold, I am cold, Andreoli! What shall we do?'

"The unfortunate men slowly descended through a layer of white clouds.

"'Hush!' said Andreoli; 'do you hear—'

"' What?' replied Zambecarri.

"'A singular noise!'

"'You are mistaken!'

"'No!—Do you see those midnight travellers, listening to that incomprehensible sound? Have they struck against a rower? Are they about to be precipitated on the roofs? Do you hear it? It is like the sound of the ocean!'

"'Impossible!'

"' It is the roaring of the waves!'

"' That is true!—Light! light!'

"After five fruitless attempts, Andreoli obtained it. It was three o'clock. The sound of the waves was heard with violence; they almost touched the surface of the sea.

"' We are lost!' exclaimed Zambecarri, seizing a bag of ballast.

"' Help!' cried Andreoli.

"The car touched the water, and the waves covered them breast high. To the sea with instruments, garments, money! The aeronauts stripped entirely. The lightened balloon rose with frightful rapidity. Zambecarri was seized with violent vomiting. Grossetti bled freely. The unhappy men could not speak; their respiration was short. They were seized with cold, and in a moment covered with a coat of ice. The moon appeared to them red as blood. After having traversed these high regions during half an hour, the machine again fell into the sea. It was four o'clock in the morning: the bodies of the wretched aeronauts were half in the water, and the balloon, acting as a sail, dragged them about during several hours. At daybreak, they found themselves opposite Pesaro, five miles from the shore; they were about to land, when a sudden flow of wind drove them back to the open sea. They were lost! The affrighted barks fled at their approach. Fortunately, a more intelligent navigator hailed them, took them on board; and they landed at Ferrara. That was frightful! Zambecarri was a brave man. Scarcely recovered from his sufferings, he recommenced his ascensions. In one of them, he struck against a tree; his lamp, filled with spirits of wine, was spilled over his clothes, and they caught fire; he was covered with flame; his machine was beginning to kindle, when he descended, half burned. The 21st September, 1812, he made another ascension at Bologna; his balloon caught in a tree; his lamp set fire to it. Zambecarri fell, and was killed! And in presence of these high facts, shall we still hesitate? No! The higher we go the more glorious will be our death."

The balloon, entirely unballasted, we were borne to incredible heights. The aerostat vibrated in the atmosphere; the slightest sound re-echoed through the celestial vaults; the globe, the only object which struck my sight in immensity, seemed about to be annihilated, and above us the heights of heaven lost themselves in the profound darkness!

I saw the unknown rise before me.

"This is the hour!" said he to me. "We must die! We are rejected by men! They despise us! let us crush them!"

"Mercy!" exclaimed I.

"Let us cut the cords! let this car be abandoned in space! The attractive force will change its direction, and we shall land in the sun!"

Despair gave me strength! I precipitated myself upon the madman, and a frightful struggle took place! But I was thrown down! and while he held me beneath his knee, he cut the cords of the car!

"One!" said he.

"Mercy! O, God!"

"Two! three!"

One cord more, and the car was sustained only on one side. I made a superhuman effort, rose, and violently repulsed this insensate.

"Four!" said he.

The car was overset. I instinctively clung to the cords which held it, and climbed up the outside.

The unknown had disappeared in space!

In a twinkling the balloon ascended to an immeasurable height! A horrible crash was heard. The dilated gas had burst its envelope! I closed my eyes. A few moments afterwards, a moist warmth reanimated me; I was in the midst of fiery clouds! The balloon was whirling with fearful rapidity! I felt myself swooning! Driven by the wind, I travelled a hundred leagues an hour in my horizontal course; the lightnings flashed around me!

Meanwhile my fall was not rapid. When I opened my eyes, I perceived the country. I was two miles from the sea, the hurricane urging me on with great force. I was lost, when a sudden shock made me let go; my hands opened, a cord slipped rapidly between my fingers, and I found myself on the ground. It was the cord of the anchor, which, sweeping the surface of the ground, had caught in a crevice! I fainted, and my lightened balloon, resuming its flight, was lost beyond the sea.

When I recovered my senses, I was in the house of a peasant, at Harderwick, a little town of Gueldre, fifteen leagues from Amsterdam, on the banks of the Zuyderzée.

A miracle had saved me. But my voyage had been but a series of imprudences against which I had been unable to defend myself.

May this terrific recital, while it instructs those who read it, not discourage the explorers of the routes of air.

www.ingramcontent.com/pod-product-compliance
Lightning Source LLC
Chambersburg PA
CBHW020819030726
47496CB00009B/2958

9 783732 624218